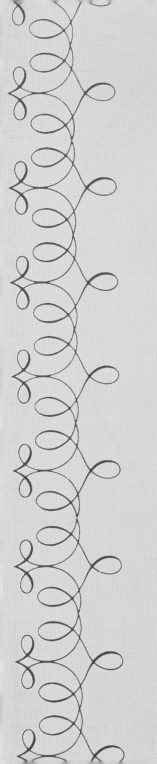
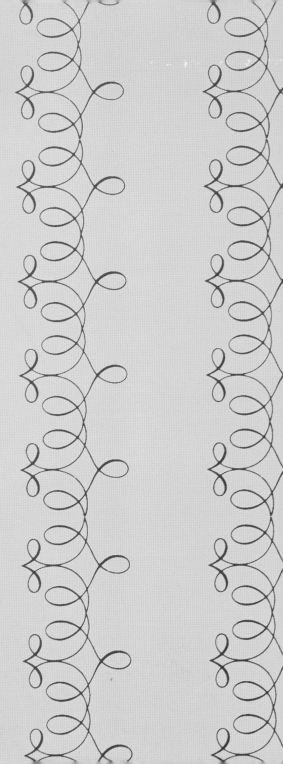
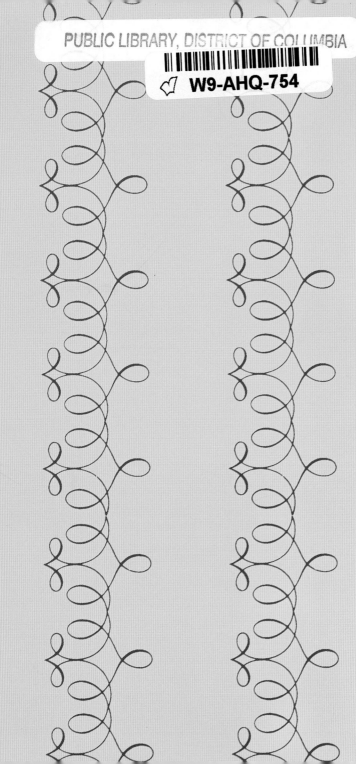

The Nutcracker

Retold by *Stephanie Spinner* · Illustrated by *Peter Malone*

With a fully orchestrated CD of the Peter Ilyich Tchaikovsky music

Alfred A. Knopf   New York

It was Christmas Eve, Marie's favorite night of the year. She was so excited that she did a pirouette on her way to the drawing room, where she joined her brother, Fritz, at the big double doors. The bustling and whispers and bursts of laughter coming from the other side meant that the grown-ups were still hanging decorations and arranging gifts.

"Isn't it time to go in yet?" asked Fritz, who was more impatient than usual tonight. Before Marie could reply, the doors swung open.

And there it was, a Christmas tree so beautiful it made their hearts thump.

As Marie and Fritz stood admiring it, a crowd of friends and relatives arrived, and there were many rounds of kisses and cordial greetings. The children said their hellos as quickly as they could and hurried to the tree, where they fell to opening their presents. Before long the drawing room rang with their joyful shrieks.

Marie and her cousins compared their new lace parasols. Fritz galloped around on his new hobbyhorse, whinnying and neighing.

Then, so suddenly that he might have been conjured, Marie's godfather, Herr Drosselmeyer, appeared. Some children were afraid of him because he was old and stiff and wore a patch over one eye, but Marie loved him. He was a little mysterious, true, but he smelled like peppermint, and he was a master toy maker. His Christmas gifts were always magical.

Now, with his nephew's help, Herr Drosselmeyer carried in three large beribboned boxes. He opened two of them and drew out a pair of life-size dolls— Harlequin and his rosy-cheeked sweetheart, Columbine. Young Drosselmeyer wound them up, and they danced together so gracefully that Marie forgot they were toys.

Herr Drosselmeyer opened the third box and out came a life-size toy soldier wearing a splendid uniform and a curlicued mustache.

Young Drosselmeyer wound him up and the soldier paraded up and down the drawing room with his eyes straight ahead. Then he performed one crisp maneuver after another, kneeling, turning, and twirling his rifle with perfect assurance. He was the very picture of a military man, and when he finally came to attention, Fritz and the other boys cheered themselves hoarse.

After Herr Drosselmeyer put away the dancing dolls, he beckoned to Marie.

"Here is something for you, my dear," he said, presenting her with a large wooden nutcracker. Though he was white-haired and dressed like a general, the nutcracker's smile was as wide and friendly as a boy's.

Marie was enchanted, especially when his handsome teeth broke open each nut she fed him with a loud, satisfying *crack*!

"Oh, Godfather!" she cried. "He's wonderful!"

"He's not!" shouted Fritz. In a sudden fit of jealousy, he snatched the nutcracker from Marie and whacked him on the floor. The nutcracker's jaw broke and three of his teeth went flying.

Marie wept. Fritz was roundly scolded. Herr Drosselmeyer bandaged the nutcracker, and Young Drosselmeyer found a bed just the right size for him. They both promised Marie that the doll would soon recover, and that cheered her. So did dancing with Young Drosselmeyer, who never once stepped on her toes.

But that night Marie dreamed that her wonderful nutcracker was attacked by a monster. She woke with her heart pounding.

"I must make sure my nutcracker is safe," she thought.

She tiptoed down to the drawing room, where she found him resting peacefully on his little bed. "Thank goodness!" she sighed. Then, overcome with drowsiness, she climbed onto the sofa and promptly fell asleep.

A clap of thunder woke her. Lightning flashed—once, twice, three times—and in its brilliance, everything in the drawing room began to change.

The Christmas tree grew and grew. So did the doors and windows. And when an army of toy soldiers marched out of their cabinet, Marie saw that they were taller than she was!

Before she could even pinch herself, the Nutcracker, now very much alive, strode over to Marie and kissed her hand.

In the next instant she heard frenzied squeaking and the *tk-tk-tk* of scurrying rodent feet.

And then the mice attacked.

Marie had always been afraid of mice. Whenever she said so, Fritz would scoff, "They're tiny! They can't hurt you!"

But these mice were big and tubby and beady-eyed, with twitchy whiskers and tails like whips. Led by their seven-headed king, they charged the soldiers.

The soldiers retaliated by firing a cannon full of cheese balls. But even this bold defense could not stop the mice from their deadly advance.

Meanwhile, the Mouse King had cornered the Nutcracker and seized his sword. "Now I've got you," he squeaked, his many eyes glittering with malice.

"Oh no, you don't!" cried Marie. Taking careful aim, she flung her slipper straight at the Mouse King, and—*thwack!*—hit him squarely on the nose. He tottered helplessly. In that instant the Nutcracker reclaimed his sword and dealt the king a mortal blow.

The mice scurried away.

The Nutcracker stood before Marie, holding one of the Mouse King's golden crowns. "You saved my life," he said, his voice breaking with gratitude.

Then, to Marie's astonishment and joy, he turned into a handsome young prince—who bore a striking resemblance to her godfather's nephew.

"Wear this, my dear Marie," he said, placing the crown on her head, "and come with me to my kingdom—the Land of Sweets."

They flew hand in hand to a forest, where the air swirled with snowflakes of purest white, and snow fairies spun before them in a welcoming dance.

As it ended, a snowflake touched Marie's lips. "It's sweet!" she cried.

"Everything in my kingdom is sweet," said the prince, smiling. "You'll see."

Soon they arrived at the prince's palace, which was made entirely of spun sugar.

The Sugar Plum Fairy, who watched over the kingdom when the prince was away, greeted them with a radiant smile. Her tiara sparkled with tiny jewels and her gown was sewn with gems of every color, but the light in her eyes shone brightest of all. She was the loveliest creature Marie had ever seen.

The fairy led them to a table piled high with exotic sweets.

"A little light refreshment—in case you are hungry," she said. "The sugar plums are especially good."

And then she summoned the court to dance in their honor.

A troupe of Spanish flamenco dancers twirled before them to the sound of castanets, clicking their heels impossibly fast.

A pair of Chinese dancers carried in a giant teapot, and out leaped a boy in silk pajamas who jumped so high, and so fast, that he might have had springs in his feet.

An Arabian dancing girl coiled and uncoiled herself to the haunting music of a single pipe. "Like a snake waking up from a nap," thought Marie.

Then came a troupe of dancers with candy canes, bounding around the hall with such exuberance that Marie expected them to fly at any moment.

In contrast, the shepherdesses were as dainty as porcelain dolls, pointing their toes and playing their pipes in a most ladylike fashion.

Madame Ginger bustled in after them, powdering her face. While she primped, a horde of little gingersnap children ran out from under her skirts, dancing as happily as if they had been let out of school.

The soaring, elegant Waltz of the Flowers followed, and when the last of the exquisite candied flowers had melted away, the Sugar Plum Fairy announced that she, too, would dance for them.

"We are truly honored," said the prince.

Marie wished the fairy's dance with her cavalier would never end, for it seemed to express everything that was heartfelt and good about Christmas. But it did end, and then it was time for Marie and the prince to say goodbye to the Land of Sweets.

"Thank you! Thank you!" they cried as they flew off in a magnificent sled drawn by reindeer.

High above his kingdom, the prince took Marie's hand. She yawned, suddenly very sleepy. As her eyes closed, she promised herself that she would never, ever forget this wondrous night.

And she never did.

A Note to the Reader

The *Nutcracker* ballet, based on E.T.A. Hoffmann's story "The Nutcracker and the Mouse King," was choreographed by Marius Petipa and Lev Ivanov to music by Peter Ilyich Tchaikovsky, and was first performed at the Mariinsky Ballet of St. Petersburg in 1892.

It was not well received. Russian critics called the production "an insult" and pronounced the Sugar Plum Fairy "podgy" and "ponderous." Only Tchaikovsky's brilliant score escaped censure. Later Russian *Nutcracker*s came in all shapes and sizes: without the first and second scenes, with Marie and the prince as adults, with an eccentric aunt taking the place of Herr Drosselmeyer, and many other changes.

Like an immigrant finding a better life far from home, *The Nutcracker* saw its fortunes improve when it came to the West. From 1915 on, some of the world's greatest ballerinas—Anna Pavlova, Alicia Markova, and Margot Fonteyn—danced the part of the Sugar Plum Fairy in shortened versions. Many renowned companies, including the Ballet Russe de Monte Carlo, toured the United States presenting the ballet in one act.

The Nutcracker became a full-length production with children in the cast when William Christensen staged it for the San Francisco Ballet in 1944. The definitive *Nutcracker* came ten years later, when George Balanchine choreographed it for the New York City Ballet. Balanchine, who had danced the part of Drosselmeyer's toy soldier as a teenager in St. Petersburg, drew on memories of the original production when creating his version. It, like Christensen's, includes very young dancers. Now every year countless young ballet students dream of becoming a mouse, a prince, or a little girl on a magical journey.

For Claude Brunson Conyers
—S.S.

For Phoebe and Imogen
—P.M.

THIS IS A BORZOI BOOK PUBLISHED BY ALFRED A. KNOPF

Text copyright © 2008 by Stephanie Spinner • Illustrations copyright © 2008 by Peter Malone

Orchestral recording of Peter Ilyich Tchaikovsky's THE NUTCRACKER by the Utah Symphony Orchestra under the direction of Maurice Abravanel, reproduced with permission.

Visit us on the Web! www.randomhouse.com/kids

Educators and librarians, for a variety of teaching tools, visit us at www.randomhouse.com/teachers

Library of Congress Cataloging-in-Publication Data
Spinner, Stephanie.
The nutcracker / retold by Stephanie Spinner ; illustrated by Peter Malone. — 1st ed.
p. cm.
Summary: In this retelling of the original 1816 German story, Godfather Drosselmeyer gives young Marie a nutcracker for Christmas, and she finds herself in a magical realm
where she saves the nutcracker and sees him change into a handsome prince.
ISBN 978-0-375-84464-5 (trade) — ISBN 978-0-375-94464-2 (lib. bdg.)
[1. Fairy tales. 2. Christmas—Fiction.] I. Malone, Peter, ill. II. Hoffmann, E. T. A. (Ernst Theodor Amadeus), 1776–1822. Nussknacker und Mausekönig. III. Title.
PZ8.S465Nut 2008   [E]—dc22   2007041524

The text of this book is set in 14-point Goudy. The illustrations in this book were created using watercolor on paper.

MANUFACTURED IN CHINA
October 2008   10 9 8 7 6 5 4 3 2 1   First Edition

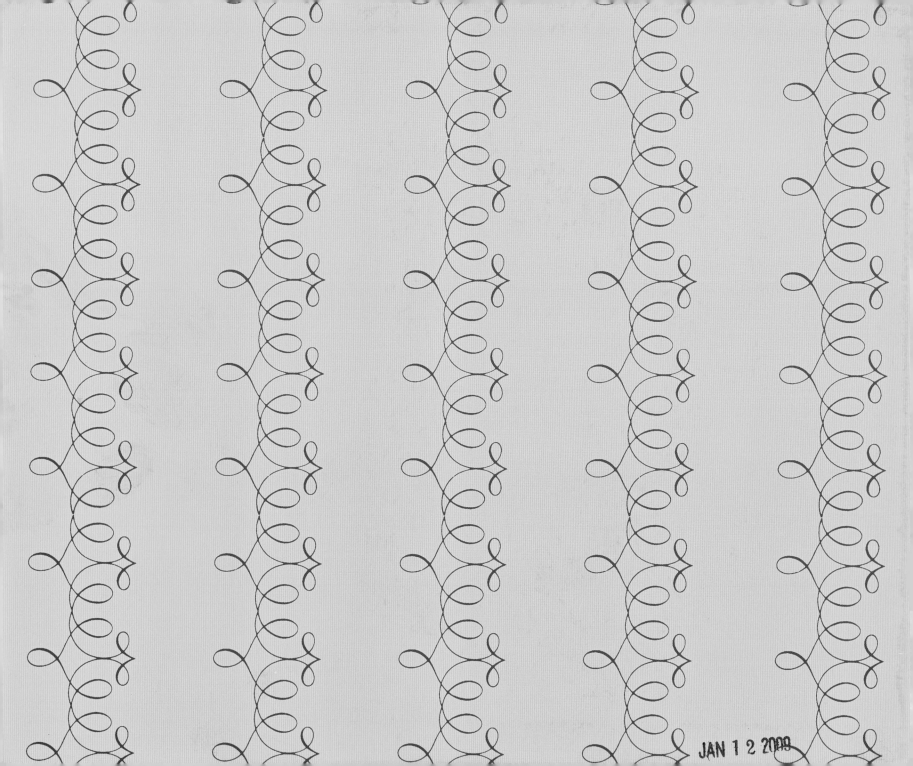